The Music Fairies

For Hannah Whitehead,
with lots of love

Special thanks to
Sue Mongredien

ORCHARD BOOKS
338 Euston Road, London NW1 3BH
Orchard Books Australia
Level 17/207 Kent Street, Sydney, NSW 2000
A Paperback Original

First published in 2008 by Orchard Books.

HiT entertainment

A CIP catalogue record for this book is available
from the British Library.

ISBN 978 1 40830 027 5

1 3 5 7 9 10 8 6 4 2

Printed in Great Britain by
CPI Cox & Wyman, Reading, RG1 8EX

Orchard Books is a division of Hachette Children's Books,
an Hachette Livre UK company

www.hachettelivre.co.uk

Victoria
the Violin
Fairy

by Daisy Meadows

ORCHARD BOOKS

www.rainbowmagic.co.uk

Jack Frost's
Ice Castle

The Park

High Street

The Alley

MUSIC SHOP

Kirsty's House

Fields ↑

Wetherbury Hotel

I'm through with frost, ice and snow.
To the human world I must go!
I'll form a cool, Gobolicious Band.
Magical instruments will lend a hand.

With these instruments I'll go far.
Frosty Jack, a superstar.
I'll steal music's harmony and fun.
Watch out world, I'll be number one!

Contents

Listen to the Band

"I like that song," Rachel Walker said, pointing at the computer screen. She and her best friend, Kirsty Tate, were downloading music from the internet, using a gift card that Rachel got for her birthday.

Kirsty nodded. "Me too," she said, clicking the mouse to download the track. Rachel was staying with Kirsty's family for a week over the autumn half term – and so far the girls had been having a very exciting time. A very musical time, too – helping the Music Fairies find their lost Magical Instruments! Mr Tate, Kirsty's dad, came into the room at that moment. "I've just been talking to my friend, Charles, on the phone," he told them. "Kirsty, do you

remember him? He works at
Wetherbury College and he's been
telling me about a really talented
band who have been
practising there. He's
sure they're going
to do well in the
National Talent
Competition
tomorrow."

Kirsty's ears pricked
up at her dad's words. She and
Rachel knew someone else who was
determined to go far in the National
Talent Competition – Jack Frost!
He was so desperate to win the
contest, he'd ordered his goblin
servants to steal the Music Fairies'
Magical Instruments, so that his group,

Frosty and his Gobolicious Band, would sound the best. Jack Frost wanted the star prize – a recording contract with MegaBig Record Company – but Kirsty and Rachel knew this would be a disaster. Once the public discovered that Jack Frost wasn't human, all the girls' fairy friends would be in danger of being discovered by curious humans!

"The band are rehearsing at the college," Mr Tate went on, "and Charles asked if we'd like to go along and listen."

"Yes, please," Kirsty said. "We'd love to!"

Mr Tate nodded. "I'll drop you there," he replied. "I can't stay myself – I've got a few errands to run."

Rachel smiled and got to her feet. "It'll be so cool if we get to see the winning band before the Talent Competition tomorrow," she said.

"And you never know," Kirsty murmured to her as Mr Tate went to get his car keys, "we might spot another of the Magical Musical Instruments while we're there..."

Rachel nodded. She and Kirsty had helped the Music Fairies find five of their missing instruments so far, but

there were still two left to discover —
the violin and the saxophone. The
Magical Instruments were very
important, because their fairy owners
used them to make music fun and
tuneful in Fairyland and throughout
the human world. While the instruments
had been missing, music just didn't
sound the same.

Mr Tate drove Kirsty
and Rachel to
Wetherbury
College, and
Charles let
them in.
"Bye, Dad,"
Kirsty said
to Mr Tate.
"See you later!"

"Thanks for this, Charles," Mr Tate said to his friend, then waved goodbye to Kirsty and Rachel. "Enjoy yourselves!"

As Charles led the girls down a corridor, his phone rang with a loud ringtone.

Charles took the call quickly as they walked along. Then he hung up and pushed a door open. "Here we are — the auditorium," he said. "In we go."

Rachel and Kirsty followed Charles
into a large hall, with a wide stage
and rows of seats. They could see four
figures on the stage with their
instruments, rehearsing a song.

"Have a seat," Charles whispered.
"You're welcome to stay for as long
as you like, provided you're quiet
and don't disturb the lads."

Kirsty and Rachel sat down at the
back of the hall, and listened to
the music. The band were playing a
lively, original tune that made Kirsty
want to dance. "They're great!" she
whispered to Rachel, tapping her feet.

"Really unusual," Rachel agreed.
"And they look so young!"

Kirsty peered at the band members,
who were quite far away in the

distance. One was playing maracas, one had a banjo, another was playing a violin and the fourth had a recorder. Rachel was right – the band didn't look much older than the two girls.

"How come those boys can play so well?" she marvelled. "That's amazing!"

A thought struck Rachel. The fairies had told the girls that the power of the Magical Musical Instruments meant that whoever played them, or was close to them, was able to produce perfect-sounding music. "I wonder if one of the Magical Instruments is nearby?" Rachel whispered to Kirsty. "That could be

why the band sound so brilliant –
because the powerful fairy magic is
helping them play like that!"

Then another thought hit her.
"Kirsty – what if the band are *goblins*?"
she whispered in alarm.

Goblins on Stage

Kirsty leaned forwards immediately to take a closer look. She and Rachel knew that Jack Frost had cast a spell over his goblins to make them blend in better with humans – so now the goblins were all boy-sized and flesh-coloured, rather than being their usual small green selves. The spell hadn't changed everything about the goblins, though. They still had big noses and large feet – and that was how Kirsty and Rachel had been able to see through their disguises so far.

The girls peered at the members of the band but it was difficult to

tell whether they were goblins or not. The auditorium was very big, and Kirsty, Rachel and Charles were right at the back. "Charles, we're just going a bit nearer the front," Kirsty whispered to him.

"Sure," he whispered back. "Great, aren't they?"

"Really good," Kirsty agreed. Then she and Rachel tiptoed through the seats, heading towards the stage so that they could see the musicians better.

It wasn't long before both girls were in no doubt. With those noses and ears, the performers on stage were definitely goblins!

Kirsty and Rachel slid into seats near the front, ducking low as the band finished their song. They didn't want to be spotted by the goblins.

"That sounded great," the goblin on the banjo said. "I'm really getting the hang of this now. Not as good as when I had that Magic Guitar, of course, but all the same... We sound brilliant, lads. Jack Frost will be really pleased next time he hears us."

"When is Jack Frost going to be at one of our rehearsals?" the goblin on the maracas asked. "I know he thinks he's such a great singer he doesn't need any practice, but I think it would be a good idea for us to rehearse together at least once or twice before the competition."

"You're right," the goblin on the recorder agreed. "But you know what the boss is like. He does things his own way. Come on, let's practise our next song."

Kirsty and Rachel could hardly breathe with excitement as they heard the goblins' conversation. So this was Frosty's Gobolicious Band – without "Frosty" himself, of course!

"There are only two Magical Instruments left to find, aren't there?" Kirsty whispered to Rachel in the tiniest voice she could manage, as the band started playing again. "Violin and saxophone. I'm pretty sure that violin must be Victoria the Violin Fairy's Magical Instrument, don't you think?"

Rachel nodded. "It must be," she agreed, whispering right into Kirsty's ear so that the goblins wouldn't hear her. "But what can we do to get it back? With Charles sitting up there listening, we can't disturb the band. He'd be cross with us – and then the goblins might get away."

27

Kirsty thought for a moment. Rachel was right – they mustn't make Charles suspicious by interrupting the rehearsal. But she and Rachel really needed to get the Magic Violin for Victoria!

As she was thinking, her gaze fell upon the footlights at the front of the stage. They were all on, shining golden light towards the band. But one of the lights was glowing with different colours, in a very magical kind of way...

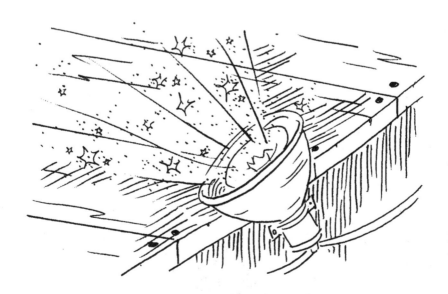

Kirsty nudged Rachel, suddenly hopeful. "Rachel, look at that multicoloured light," she whispered. "I think it might be a fairy!"

Ring! Ring!

Kirsty and Rachel glanced up at where Charles was sitting. His eyes were shut and he was leaning back in his seat, engrossed in the music. "Let's investigate," Rachel whispered back.

The two friends carefully made their way towards the footlights, hiding in the shadows as they went.

Suddenly a small cloud of colourful sparkles rose up from the footlight, and a tiny fairy appeared, listening to the music with her head on one side.

She had long dark hair and wore a pretty T-shirt decorated with a butterfly pattern, and jeans tucked into cowboy boots. The girls recognised her immediately from when they'd met all the Music Fairies at the beginning of this adventure. "It's Victoria!" Kirsty murmured happily, smiling in delight to see their fairy friend once more.

The girls tiptoed up to Victoria. "Hi there," Rachel whispered.

Victoria beamed as she saw Rachel. "Hello," she said in a silvery voice. "I'm so glad to see you. Those goblins have got my violin, and I really need it back!"

Kirsty slid to the floor in front of the stage, where she'd be out of sight, and motioned for Rachel and Victoria to do the same. "Hi Victoria," she said softly.

"We guessed that might be your violin
– we recognised the goblins and
thought their playing was too good to
be true!"

"The only thing is," Rachel added,
"we'll have to get a man called Charles
out of here before we try anything with
the goblins. He's sitting at the back of
the auditorium
listening, and told
us we mustn't
disturb the
band," she
explained to
Victoria.

Kirsty suddenly
remembered how
loud Charles's ringtone
had been when he'd had a call earlier.

"If he had a phone call, he'd have to
go out of the room!" she said
thoughtfully. "I wonder if we could get
his number somehow and
call him…"

Victoria
smiled. "Or
I could make
his phone ring
with my
wand," she
suggested. "And
I'll use some special
fairy magic to make sure that when
Charles answers his phone, there'll be
a voice at the other end to keep him
chatting for a while!"

Rachel and Kirsty grinned. "Great!"
Rachel said. "Let's try it."

Victoria pointed her wand up towards where Charles was sitting, and flicked it deftly. The air shimmered with magic, then Charles's ringtone sounded through the auditorium. He jumped up, patting his pockets frantically to find his phone.

"Sorry – so sorry!" he called down to the band, looking flustered and embarrassed. He rushed out at once, the phone to his ear.

The goblins stopped playing, and looked annoyed at the disturbance.

"Shall we start that one again from the top?" the goblin with the maracas suggested.

The goblin with the violin shook his head. "I want to practise *Goblin Serenade* now," he said.

"Not again!" the goblin with the recorder moaned. "We've rehearsed that one loads of times already!"

"He only wants to play that one because he's got his long violin solo in the middle of it," the goblin with the banjo said sourly.

"That's why I need to practise it, banjo-brain!" the violinist retorted.

While the goblins argued, Rachel, Kirsty and Victoria discussed in whispers what to do next. "We'll have a better chance of getting the Magic Violin if we can somehow separate the goblin violinist from the others," Rachel said. "Otherwise we'll be outnumbered."

Kirsty had an idea. "How about if we shine a light at the front of the stage?" she said slowly, thinking as she spoke. "If the violinist has a solo, he will probably step into the spotlight. And when he does, we could lower one of the scenery backdrops down behind him, cutting him off from his friends!"

Victoria grinned. "And when he's on his own, we can get my violin!" she laughed. "Kirsty, that's brilliant!"

Rachel was smiling too. "Good idea," she said, gazing at the side of the stage. "It looks as if we'll be able to lower the backdrop by pulling on those ropes there — see?"

"And I can turn on and position the spotlight with my magic," Victoria added. "It's a great plan!"

The goblins had started playing another song by now, and the girls sneaked to the side of the stage and hid in the curtain folds.

Victoria was hovering
above them and as soon
as the goblin with
the violin

began his solo, she waved
her wand at the central
spotlight above the stage. The
spotlight swivelled then turned
itself on, shining a pool of light
at the very front of the stage.
The goblin with the violin looked
delighted and walked
forwards to stand
in the centre
of the light. He
shut his eyes and
continued to
play beautifully.

The lilting melody sent shivers down
Kirsty's spine. The violin had to be very
magical indeed, she thought to herself,
to enable the lumpy-fingered goblin to
produce such fantastic music!

"I think this is the rope, Kirsty,"
Rachel said just then, putting her hands
on the thick brown cord that dangled
from the top of the curtains.

"If we both pull on it, we should be able to lower the scenery panel – and separate the goblins."

Kirsty took hold of the rope too and looked at Rachel. "Ready?" she whispered. "One, two, three...PULL!"

Curtain Call

The two friends held their breath as they heaved on the rope. Would their plan work?

"Oh, yes!" cheered Rachel softly as the scenery panel fell down behind the violinist. Now he was completely cut off from his friends.

The backdrop that hung behind the goblin showed a winter wonderland scene, with snowy mountain peaks and ice-skaters on a frozen lake. The girls could hear the rest of the band shouting through the panel to their friend. "How did that happen? Are you all right, mate?" they called.

The goblin playing the violin was so wrapped up in his music, he didn't notice their shouts and went on playing, his eyes shut as he picked out the melody.

"Charles might be back at any moment," Rachel remembered just then. "Should we close the main curtains too, do you think? That way the goblin with the violin will be trapped between the curtains and the scenery, and Charles won't be able to see what's happening if he walks in."

"Good idea," Victoria said and waved her wand. Red sparkles crackled from its tip and glittery fairy magic streamed out all over the heavy, velvety curtains. Moments later, they had magically swung closed in front of the goblin.

Kirsty, Rachel and Victoria went quietly onto the stage, taking care not to disturb the musician. "You'd better stay out of sight," Kirsty told Victoria.

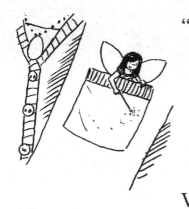

"We'll have a better chance of getting the violin if the goblin doesn't know we're with you."

"You're right," Victoria said, tucking herself into Kirsty's pocket. "I'll hide in here."

Just as her gauzy wings vanished from view, the goblin stopped playing and opened his eyes. Then he blinked and stared around in confusion. Even with the light shining down on him, it was much darker on the stage now that the curtains were shut.

"Bravo!" Kirsty shouted loudly, trying to drown out the cries of the other goblins behind the backdrop. "Fantastic!"

Rachel clapped as hard as she could.

"That was wonderful," she agreed, stepping nearer to the goblin.

The goblin bowed, but in doing so, he noticed the snowy backdrop behind him and straightened immediately, looking puzzled. He shivered. "How did I get outside?" he wondered in confusion. "Are my friends hiding in the snow?"

"It's just scenery," Kirsty replied, thinking swiftly. "You're not really outside. We're…we're the stagehands, you see. Sorry about that, the scenery panel fell down by mistake. I'll hold the violin for you while you go under it, if you like."

Clever Kirsty! Rachel was impressed by her friend's quick wits, and backed her up at once. "Yes, your friends are just on the other side of this picture," she added.

The violin-playing goblin looked from Kirsty to Rachel to the backdrop, still frowning. "Lads, are you there?" he shouted. "I'll be with you in a minute. Stay where you are."

51

Then he looked down at his violin and clutched it a little tighter. "I'll keep hold of this, though," he told the girls haughtily. "It's a very valuable instrument, this violin of mine."

"Huh!" sniffed Victoria from her hiding place in Kirsty's pocket. Kirsty guessed she didn't like the way the goblin had referred to the violin as belonging to *him*.

Rachel pretended she was struggling to raise the backdrop. "It's...very...heavy," she panted, letting it fall again. "We won't be able to lift it very high. I'm afraid you're going to have to crawl on the floor to get under it."

The goblin looked appalled. "Crawl?" he echoed. "World-class musicians don't crawl, thank you very much! Don't you know who you're talking to? Future winner of the National Talent Competition, that's who!" He drew himself up to his full height, and puffed out his chest. "Besides, I can't possibly crawl through there with my violin," he went on. "It might get scratched or damaged – I can't let that happen."

"Well, that's why I offered to hold it for you," Kirsty said. "And then, once you're safely through on the other side, I'll pass it to you. I promise I'll be careful."

The goblin considered this for a moment but then shook his head. "No," he said, holding the violin protectively against him. "I can't risk it. I don't want anyone else touching my precious instrument."

"*His* precious instrument indeed," Victoria muttered darkly from Kirsty's pocket. Kirsty had to pretend to cough so that the goblin didn't hear.

The goblin edged slowly towards the backdrop. "I'm going to put my violin down on the floor, crawl under the scenery backwards, then pick it up when I'm on the other side," he decided. Then he glared at the girls. "And you'd better not try any funny business," he added suspiciously. "I'll be keeping a close eye on you!"

Two Violins

"Of course," Rachel said politely, although her mind was whirling. How were they going to get the violin?

Then, out of the corner of her eye, she spotted a cardboard box full of instruments at the edge of the stage. Someone had written "Wetherbury College Orchestra" on the side of the box, and there on the top lay a violin.

Rachel's eyes widened in surprise as she saw it. What a stroke of luck! It had given her an idea that might just work...

"Victoria," she whispered, moving closer to Kirsty so that she could attract the attention of the little fairy, "would you be able to use your magic to turn out the lights when the goblin puts down his violin? Because we might be able to do a little swap in the dark..."

Victoria peeked over the edge of Kirsty's pocket and her eyes brightened when she saw the second violin at which Rachel was gesturing. "No problem," Victoria whispered back, giving a thumbs-up sign. "Good thinking, Rachel!"

Kirsty took hold of the scenery panel and looked at the goblin. "Ready when you are," she said to him. Rachel, meanwhile, slipped over to the box of instruments and hid the ordinary violin behind her back.

The goblin put the Magic Violin on the floor and got down on his hands and knees. Rachel took a step nearer to him and he scowled.

"You stay there," he ordered her.
"I don't trust either of you two!"

Rachel stopped obediently, and the
goblin began to crawl backwards under
the backdrop. As soon as his head was
through, Victoria waved her wand
quickly – and out went the lights!

The stage was now plunged into
darkness. "What's happening?" the
goblin bellowed furiously, but Rachel

had no time to answer. Her heart beating, she reached down to where the goblin had left the Magic Violin and grabbed it, deftly exchanging it for the ordinary one. Quickly, she stepped away again — just as she heard the goblin's hand groping around on the floor. "Ahh — here it is," she heard him say, his voice muffled. "Come here, my beauty — I've got you now."

There was a faint clattering as he dragged the ordinary violin under the backdrop. "Ha!" the girls and Victoria heard him shout triumphantly. "You might have tried to trick me, turning off the lights like that, but I've still got my violin!"

"Oh no, he hasn't," Rachel whispered, stumbling through the darkness back to Kirsty and Victoria.

"It's right here!" Victoria flicked on the lights again with a wave of her wand, and Kirsty, who'd been holding up the scenery panel,

let it drop as she saw that the goblin
had vanished to the other side of
it. Victoria clapped her
hands in delight at
the sight of her
Magic Violin in
Rachel's hand.
"Well done!" she
cheered, fluttering
over excitedly. "That
worked perfectly, girls!"

The sound of the violinist goblin's
voice came through the backdrop loud
and clear as he spoke to his friends.
"There were some girls there who were
trying to trick me and get the Magic
Violin, you know, but don't worry!"
he said. "I wasn't going to fall for their
silly tricks — I've still got it right here."

Then came the sound of violin-playing – a rather tuneless, scraping noise that made Victoria cover her ears. The music from the ordinary violin wasn't awful – it was still close enough to Victoria's Magic Violin to prevent that – but it didn't sound anywhere near as good as the music the goblin had played earlier.

"That's not right," the girls heard him say in a puzzled voice. There was a long pause and then the truth seemed to dawn on him. "Hey! I *have* been tricked. Those girls have stolen my violin!"

"Let's get it back!" came a furious shout from another goblin. "Quick!"

And then, to the girls' dismay, goblin arms and legs began appearing under the backdrop as the goblin band struggled to scramble through.

Kirsty and Rachel both pulled at the velvet curtains at the front of the stage, trying to escape. But the material was thick and hung in gathered folds, and neither of them could find the opening.

"Victoria, help!" Kirsty cried, feeling panicky. "We're going to be trapped!"

Fly Away!

Victoria flung a handful of fairy dust over the girls and they immediately shrank down to fairy-size – as did the Magic Violin, still in Rachel's grasp. "Follow me," Victoria called out, fluttering her wings hard so that she flew straight up in the air.

Kirsty and Rachel copied her,
zooming upwards just as the goblins
came under the backdrop, tumbling
onto the centre of the stage.

Victoria waved her wand at the
curtains, and they swung open just wide
enough for the three fairy friends to fly
through. Kirsty looked over her shoulder
to see the curtains close themselves
again – and then bulges appeared in
the material as the goblins tried to fight
their way through.

"This is all YOUR fault!" one yelled.

"Why did you let those girls get that violin?"

"They tricked me — how was I to know?" came the angry reply.

"Jack Frost will go mad when he hears about this!" a third goblin wailed. "I suppose we'd better go back and break the news."

The curtains went still and there was some furious muttering, which Kirsty and Rachel couldn't make out. Then there came the sound of the goblins stomping away, still bickering.

The girls and Victoria held their breath for a few moments, but all was silent in the auditorium.

"I think they've gone," Victoria said in relief. She led the girls to perch on one of the auditorium seats, her eyes shining with happiness as Rachel handed over the precious Magic Violin. Blue sparkles flashed all around it, and Victoria smiled. "Thank you so much," she said gratefully. "Now that I have my violin again, music will sound even

better throughout Fairyland and in your world." She rested the violin under her chin and played a few notes, and Kirsty and Rachel smiled in delight at the beautiful melody.

"I'd better turn you back to your
normal size now," Victoria said,
and waved her wand over them both.
The air was filled with glittering fairy
magic, and Kirsty and Rachel found
themselves getting bigger and bigger,
until they towered over Victoria as
girls once more.

"I guess we'd better look out for
Charles," Kirsty said. "It's nearly time
for us to go home."

"Let me just tidy up first," Victoria
said, pointing her wand at the stage
and muttering some magic words. The
curtains swung open to reveal the
backdrop lifting back up to the roof of
the stage, and the ordinary violin flying
back to the instrument box. "There,"
she said. "Thanks again. And do watch

out for the Magic Saxophone. It's the only instrument Jack Frost has now, so he'll be guarding it closely."

"We'll keep a lookout," Rachel promised. "Bye, Victoria. That was great fun!"

"Bye, girls," she said. "I'll take my violin back to Fairyland where it belongs!" And with a flurry of violin music, she disappeared.

Just then, the auditorium doors opened and Charles came in. "What happened to the band?" he asked, seeing the empty stage.

Kirsty and Rachel exchanged glances. "They had to go," Rachel replied truthfully.

"I've just been speaking to your dad on the phone, by the way," Charles said. "He's coming here to collect you."

"Thanks, Charles," Kirsty said. "I really enjoyed listening to the music."

The two friends went out to the college car park to meet Mr Tate. "I can't believe it's the National Talent Competition tomorrow," Rachel said as they walked. "We've got to find the Magic Saxophone as soon as possible."

Kirsty nodded. "And we must stop Jack Frost from winning the competition," she added. "I think we're in for another *fairy* busy day, Rachel!"

Now Rachel and Kirsty must help

Sadie the Saxophone Fairy

Sadie's Magic Saxophone is the last instrument for Rachel and Kirsty to find! Can they outwit the goblins before Jack Frost and his Gobolicious Band win the talent competition...?

The Competition Begins

"We'd better hurry, Kirsty," Rachel Walker said to her best friend, Kirsty Tate, as they jumped out of the car. "The talent competition will be starting soon!"

The girls waved at Mrs Tate, who had just dropped them off, and then they hurried into the New Harmony Shopping Mall.

"Good afternoon, everyone," said a voice over the loudspeaker system as the girls went inside. "The auditions for the National Talent Competition are about to start, so please make your way to the north end of the shopping mall."

Rachel and Kirsty glanced at each other as they wove their way through the crowds.

"There are lots of people here, aren't there?" Kirsty said anxiously. "I hope we get Sadie's Magic Saxophone back before Frosty and his Gobolicious Band take the stage!"

The girls had been asked by their friends, the Music Fairies, to help them find their seven Magical Musical instruments, which had been stolen from Fairyland's Royal School of Music by Jack Frost and his goblin servants. The Magical Musical Instruments were extremely important because they made music joyful and harmonious for everyone in both the human and fairy worlds. Since the instruments had gone missing, music everywhere had been ruined.

But Jack Frost had his own plans for the Magical Musical Instruments. Along with his goblin servants, he had formed a pop group called Frosty and his Gobolicious Band, and he intended to use the magical powers of the instruments to win first prize in the National Talent Competition. Rachel and Kirsty had managed to return six of the Magical Musical Instruments to Fairyland, but they were still looking for Sadie's saxophone. And the girls knew that time was running out...

Win Karaoke Machines and Dance Mats!

Have you ever wanted to be a top musician like
Ellie the Guitar Fairy or a dancing queen like
Tasha the Tap Dance Fairy? Now's your chance
to shine like a star!

We have 5 Karaoke Machines and 5 Dance Mats
to give away in our special Rainbow Magic competition*.
All you have to do is answer the questions below:

What is the name of the fairy in the
first Rainbow Magic book?

Complete this sparkly sentence in 25 words or less.
I love Rainbow Magic because...

Send your entry on a postcard to
Rainbow Magic Karaoke Competition, Orchard Books,
338 Euston Road, London NW1 3BH

* Closing date: 31st December 2008. Five winners will be drawn
at random and notified by 30th Jan 2009. For terms and
conditions please see **www.hachettechildrens.co.uk/terms**

The Music Fairies

Win Rainbow Magic goodies!

In every book in the Rainbow Magic Music Fairies series (books 64–70) there is a hidden picture of a musical note with a secret letter in it. Find all seven letters and rearrange them to make a special Music Fairies word, then send it to us. Each month we will put the entries into a draw and select one winner to receive a Rainbow Magic Sparkly T-shirt and Goody Bag!

Send your entry on a postcard to Rainbow Magic Music Fairies Competition, Orchard Books, 338 Euston Road, London NW1 3BH. Australian readers should write to Hachette Children's Books, Level 17/207 Kent Street, Sydney, NSW 2000. New Zealand readers should write to Rainbow Magic Competition, 4 Whetu Place, Mairangi Bay, Auckland, NZ. Don't forget to include your name and address. Only one entry per child. Final draw: 30th September 2009.

Good luck!

Have you checked out the

website at:
www.rainbowmagic.co.uk

Look out for the Magical Creature Fairies!

ASHLEY
THE DRAGON FAIRY
978-1-40830-349-8

LARA
THE BLACK CAT FAIRY
978-1-40830-350-4

ERIN
THE FIREBIRD FAIRY
978-1-40830-351-1

RIHANNA
THE SEAHORSE FAIRY
978-1-40830-352-8

SOPHIA
THE SNOW SWAN FAIRY
978-1-40830-353-5

LEONA
THE UNICORN FAIRY
978-1-40830-354-2

CAITLIN
THE ICE BEAR FAIRY
978-1-40830-355-9

Available
April 2009